The Spike Camp

By Travis Stepper

1

Luke checked the settings on the welder, and then set to work on the two sample slabs, sparks bouncing off the lens shade of his helmet. He examined the weld and then increased the wire feed. Turning again to the practice metal, he spread the weld across with a uniform, even bead that made the sound of sizzling bacon. His coworker Frank stepped into the room, closing the curtain to block the blinding light from the rest of the shop.

"It may sound like you're frying bacon, but it smells like crap in here," he said, rolling up the outside door.

"Whatever. You're just jealous that it's my Friday," Luke replied.

His workday would not end until he finished piecing together a batch of pipe fittings, so he picked the first two out of the bin and got started. He preplanned his movements, making sure to minimize any needless actions. A few hours later, his work space was cleaned up, the pile of finished fittings in the bin. He clocked out and booked it across the parking lot.

Luke ran through his mental checklist again, ticking off the items he had packed in his truck before driving to work that morning. All he had left to do was get groceries and gas. He generally bought the same things every time he went out, so he rolled the grocery cart through the aisles of the store on his usual loop.

He propelled himself forward with his right foot while steering with his left on the cart's frame. This attracted a few dirty looks from some of the other more self-respecting customers, but he maintained a polite distance and didn't let it bother him. Rolling into one of the emptier checkout lanes, he exchanged hellos with the checker and set about separating his groceries into refrigerated and unrefrigerated piles on the belt.

"Have a good one, man." He smiled as the cashier waved him out to the parking lot.

Luke propped open the door to the truck camper with a shovel, climbed over his gear, and started playing Tetris with the food in the cooler until he realized he had forgotten ice. As he was negotiating his way back over the gear, a gust of wind knocked the shovel down and slammed the door shut, leaving him to climb out in the dark.

Returning to his truck after purchasing ice, Luke pulled out of the parking lot. As he pulled onto the interstate, his phone buzzed. Sean. He was one of Luke's buddies from the service. They had gone through basic training together and had been bros ever since. Luke punched the answer button and brought the phone to his ear.

"Luke, you going to hunt some deer this week?"

"If I haven't got one yet, then definitely I'm going up there now," Luke replied with a snicker.

"Well, aren't you all special, taking a week off. You're not going to shoot any—"

Beep-beep-beep! The sound of a forklift backing drowned out Sean's words.

"Are you driving right now?" Luke asked.

"Yeah. It's fine. I have Bluetooth so I won't get caught," Sean replied. "If we get a bunch of snow, do you want to try out that new spot on the east si—" Sean's words were cut off by other voices. "Shit! I'll call you Friday," he said, hanging up.

There wasn't a time when Luke hadn't hunted. From shooting birds off the back porch with a BB gun to stalking elk and bear in the backcountry, hunting was part of his life. Some people emphasized the killing aspect of hunting, but he was more fascinated by the skill and knowledge required to sneak past the superhuman eyesight of a goose or the acute hearing of an elk. He relished the constantly changing physical and mental challenges that tested his strength and will: the feeling of walking into camp at one o'clock in the morning with that last elk quarter on the pack frame or freezing your balls off in a treestand all day and finally having a buck walk into your shooting lane at dusk. That was why he hunted.

A sudden bump and the growl of tires on gravel, and Luke was in the woods. He glanced back to see the orange glow lighting the dark clouds around the town behind him. Ahead, everything except his headlights was consumed by trees. Large flakes of falling snow crossed the beams as the Chevy gained elevation. Not surprisingly for a snowy Sunday night, he didn't see any animals or campers on the way up. He parked in his usual spot, then shut down the engine, leaving the auxiliary power on for the radio, rocking out to the remainder of "Holy Diver" and resting his eyes.

As the cab started to cool, he got out his gloves and lowered the camper jacks until they were level. After making a few trips to the cab to transfer excess gear from the back, Luke climbed into the camper. His camper didn't have electricity, but the propane stove heated the ceiling to ninety degrees with the floor at a comfortable forty. Not wanting to burn propane lantern mantles, he put his largest flashlight inside a yellow grocery bag, which refracted the beam on the plastic and lit the camper with a healthy glow.

Luke formed an assembly line of sandwich materials, building three ham sandwiches for the next day: lunch, dinner, and an extra. He disliked sandwiches, but they were convenient. The only thing he liked about the bread was it kept the good parts from making a mess. Along with jerky and some snacks, he also stashed a Coke, Gatorade, and two quarts of water. His survival and hunting gear was still ready from his last trip, so he set his daypack in the corner and shut off the light.

2

The insistent beeping of his alarm shattered Luke's unconsciousness. A fuzzy sense of complete ease and comfort made him question every reason he had against going back to sleep until noon. He wasn't starving. If he didn't shoot a deer, he'd be just fine. Hunting wasn't a way to save money on meat. On the other hand, he wouldn't forgive himself if he missed out on a morning hunt with fresh snow. Tag soup never tasted good, and it would be nice to keep the amount of beef he ate to a minimum—dang hormones and skittles or whatever else they gave cattle. He compromised by leaning across the camper, lighting the stove, and hitting the snooze button. His second alarm went off, and he shifted gears- every movement a struggle, he began preparing breakfast and setting out the remainder of his gear.

Everything ready, he locked the camper up, shouldered his pack and gun sling, and stepped into the forest. Four inches of powder on the ground cushioned his footsteps and muffled the snap of any twigs that weren't saturated. Luke checked his watch: 4:48 a.m. That gave him just under a half hour to get to the clear-cut on the hillside before sunrise without making too much noise. There were only stars out, but his path was easily navigable with the contrast between snow and forest.

Clumps of snow falling off the branches of a large tree drew Luke's attention to an area a hundred yards uphill. It was too cold for snow to be melting and there was no wind. Something had moved. Luke breathed as silently as he could while listening for a couple minutes. It was still too dark to shoot or identify anything, and whatever was up there would see him if he went directly through the clear-cut, so he slowly worked his way along the edge. Time was on his side. Slower meant quieter, and every minute that passed meant he could see a little better.

By the time he had moved fifty yards up the side of the clear-cut, it was light enough to see around the more open areas. He had to be getting close to where the snow had fallen from the branch. Glancing at his scope to make sure it was clear of snow and on 3X power, he stepped over a log and stood beneath a tree to listen. A wall of black rose from the brush and saplings not twenty feet away. A cow moose.

She took a couple of curious steps towards him. Her nostrils flared to catch his scent. Moose always made him nervous, but Luke stood his ground, reminding himself that they had terrible eyesight and he was downwind. Still, he took a mental inventory of all the nearby trees he could dodge behind. The moose having apparently figured out what he was, stalked off along the top of the clear-cut. Luke's relief was twofold. Not only was she out of his way, but she also didn't wake the entire forest up by thundering off.

At the top of the ridge, the clear-cut gave way to steeper, brushier terrain. Luke slung his rifle vertically across one shoulder and used his hands to pull himself along, maintaining three points of contact with each step. Careful to avoid working up a sweat that would freeze later, he took a break and turned, looking down at how far he had progressed up the mountainside.

The morning fog had not yet burnt off, and the sun shone brightly on the rolling hilltops that spread across the river valley. As his breathing returned to normal, he heard the steady whooshing sound from the stream below. Higher up the mountainside, the yellow-green tamarack needles were scattered about on the snow. Luke continued making his way upward.

The side of the ridge started to level out as he neared the top, so he slowed his pace, pausing every few steps to scan for signs of deer. A brown horizontal line behind an evergreen sapling caught his eye. Luke peered through his scope but saw only a deer-shaped log with dead brush around it. The sight did nothing to discourage him; seeing deer decoys is a fact of life when hunting.

At the top of the ridge, he turned and

began looking around for game trails that followed the ridge up and down the mountain. Sure enough, a set of deer tracks wound their way up the opposite side into a clearing through trees and brush. The snow distorted the size of the tracks, but they still revealed the deer's direction, and it was clear they had been there since last night. He stepped under a tree for cover and checked the wind with a piece of lichen from a nearby branch.

The trees on the left side of the ridge, the side that Luke had climbed, were short and dense all the way up. Along the deer trail on the other side, the trees were larger with short bushes of kinnikinic growing throughout. He decided to hunt his way up that side to avoid making noise fighting through the thicker brush. The less-dense growth was probably why the deer had chosen that route in the first place.

Snacking on some jerky, he picked his way up the mountain: Take a couple of steps, stop, look around, listen, then wait another minute longer than necessary just because. Look around again, take a couple more steps, then do it all over again. Luke made steady progress for the next hour and a half, still taking care not to break a sweat in the cold weather. He could see the end of the ridge about two-thirds of the way up the mountain where it flattened out into a wide bowl-shaped area to the right. Two other peaks enclosed the left side.

The deer tracks joined two other sets before they veered off down the mountain on their own. In the center of a stand of tamarack, Luke walked past a fresh deer bed, a freshly melted oval shape in the snow. Somewhere down the side of the mountain, a raven quorked. Luke rolled up down his glove to check his watch: 10:23 a.m. Time for an early lunch before he got to the better hunting.

He looked around for a place to eat. His gaiters kept the snow off his fleece camo pants below the knee, but they wouldn't keep his ass dry if he just sat in the snow.

Luke scraped snow off a fallen log with the back of his glove. Then he pulled a waterproof foam pad out from against his pack's backing and used that for a seat. He ate his sandwich and drank some water, making sure to push the excess air out of the bottle to prevent it from making a sloshing sound while he hunted. He packed up his gear, then glanced around to make sure he hadn't left anything.

As he climbed higher, a warm breeze knocked some of the snow off the trees. The snow was losing its powder-like consistency and getting heavier, making the rubber soles of his boots squeak every so often. Reaching the top of the ridge, he slowed down to scan his shooting lanes before changing his line of sight as the terrain flattened out. The deer trail was no longer visible on the ridge, but a deer rub had left a fresh wound on a young sapling. The deer's antlers had scraped off the bark, leaving curled tendrils along the side of the tree and in the snow where it had stomped around.

The buck's tracks trailed down the side of the mountain. Luke passed them, contouring the side of the bowl roughly a hundred feet from the edge where the trees were less dense. A tan form sprang from the brush twenty yards away, bounding off with its white tail flagging through the air as a warning for other deer in the area. Luke stopped short and reactively brought his rifle into a more ready position, but he saw no antlers. He glanced from side to side, listening for any other sounds coming from the brush.

Another doe went trotting off in the same direction as the first. This one looked a little calmer, now that it knew the location of the threat. He heard the first one snorting four or five hundred yards away, and the second doe moved with it to the other side of the small basin. Luke leaned against a nearby tree for ten minutes, listening. The wind had brought in more clouds, and it looked like it might snow. No bucks yet, but they were definitely here.

3

Luke stretched, his back and shoulders sore from standing with a daypack all morning. It was 12:22 p.m., and the forest had been quiet since the does had run off. He continued to the edge of the basin, now about halfway along its edge. Rutting bucks had marked their territory, rubbing and scraping the trees and the ground. When he saw two sets of wolf tracks, he paused. "That isn't going to help my chances any" he inferred. The snow was shallow enough for him to believe that the prints weren't distorted in size. Luke crouched down to measure the prints. He curled his fingers to the second knuckle and pressed his palm against the track. The print matched the outline of his hand.

Cinching his pack tighter, he continued walking. He pointed threateningly at a squirrel as it chattered while he passed by its tree. Cursing under his breath, Luke slowly made his way out of the squirrel's territory where his presence would be less obvious.

Large flakes of snow began to fall, slowly blanketing the trees overhead. Digging into the side of his pack, he pulled out his scope cover and put the plastic cups over each end to keep out the snow and fog. He could still see through the plastic lenses, but for longer shots, he would need to take off the whole cover.

Luke knocked the snow off a tree branch as he walked by. Making sure a branch was free of snow before brushing up against it was a trick he had learned to keep gear dry when traveling. He grinned, remembering how his perspective of bad weather in the woods had changed after learning that trick. His reverie was interrupted when, off to his left towards the center of the basin, a branch moved. Luke peered through the screen of steadily falling snowflakes and realized that the branch was the right antler of a small forked-horn buck standing behind an uprooted stump not ten yards away.

The buck hadn't seen him yet, but with only the tops of his antlers showing, he didn't have any sort of shot. Luke mentally assessed the readiness of his rifle; he needed to make as few movements as possible. He had left the scope in 3X power that morning. He would leave the cover on or it would make too much noise or the lens could fog before he could get a shot. Three steps to the right with his gun shouldered and he would have a clear view. He was fine with shooting a small buck; Luke was out for dinner and couldn't be too choosy this far into the season.

He pushed the gun sling forward up

the stock to prevent it from moving or making sound and simultaneously hooked his right thumb against the bolt, ensuring that the round was still completely chambered. He pushed the safety on the trigger guard to off, using his index finger and thumb on both sides to prevent that click it always seems to make while keeping an eye on the deer's antlers. They were bobbing around as if he were feeding, not stock-still or side to side as if alarmed or alert.

Shouldering the rifle, he looked through the scope. A third of the lens was covered with snow but the rest was clear and unfogged. He took a step to the side with his right foot. The fresh snow and the light wind kept noise to a minimum. The tops of the buck's ears were now visible, and Luke took another step, this time with his left foot. No change from the deer. He stepped to the right again. His boot went through the snow, hitting a buried beargrass stalk. He stopped midstep and held his balance, his eyes on the deer.

A space between the gnarled roots of the stump offered a direct line of sight between Luke and the deer's heart and lungs. Through his scope, Luke saw flakes of snow melting on individual shoulder hairs. He took a breath, exhaled halfway, and paused. Something looked off. Its head faced the same way as its elbow, even though its neck wasn't turned.

Crunch. A bit of the beargrass broke down under his right boot before he shifted his weight to keep from breaking the rest. The buck turned towards the noise, stepping around from behind the roots of the stump, a doe at his side. The deer hadn't seen him, but they took a couple of steps forward. The doe was directly in line with his shot at the buck. Luke slowly moved his gun over to keep his movement undetectable. His arms and left leg were about to give out from balancing for so long, but he kept his stance. The buck walked another twenty yards towards the edge of the basin and then moved out of sight. The doe remained in

Luke's line of fire.

With the deer out of sight, Luke relaxed. He checked his watch. It was already 2:48.Luke planned to hunt the basin until dark and then walk down the ridge back to camp. The deer hadn't spooked badly, so he decided to continue after them in hopes of a clear shot. He brushed the snow out of his scope cover and began painstakingly following the deer trail, making sure to look into each new shooting lane that came into view.

The brush thickened as he neared the far side of the basin, but he kept tracking. It was easy, since the older prints were filling up with snow. When Luke saw an end to the trees ahead, he knew he had reached the far side of the bowl. He paused alongside some dead standing timber and watched a small bird peck around the bark.

Looking over the side of the basin, Luke saw the forked-horn buck and his doe grazing a hundred yards downhill at the edge of a dirt patch that had eroded out of the hillside. As he positioned himself against a nearby tree to get a more accurate shot, his peripheral vision caught the movement of lichen waving in the wind. He turned his head to the side. A massive buck was bedded down in some low brush, checking out the forked horn's doe. Then it saw Luke.

The buck sprang to its feet and

hurled itself towards the edge of the slide. Luke pushed off from the side of the tree with his elbow and brought his gun to bear. He lined it up through the trees, moving evenly with the running buck. Boom! The bullet, aimed right behind the buck's shoulder, left the muzzle of the gun, clipped a twig, and veered off into the front of its left shoulder.

The buck leaped in the air and disappeared down the mountainside. Knowing that he had hit the deer but not knowing how badly it was injured, Luke noted the last place he had seen it and waited ten minutes. Hunters often run up to a deer they have hit, only to have it jump up in a rush of adrenaline and run another mile instead of passing on quietly at its original spot. Luke used the time to mentally give thanks and respect not only for but to the deer as well.

While he waited, he ate his second sandwich and drank a Gatorade. The work had just begun. As he packed up, Luke put the expended cartridge in his empty sandwich bag. He didn't like to litter, nor did he want the smell of gunpowder on his hunting gear.

4

Grabbing brush to steady himself, Luke slid down the embankment to where he had last seen the buck. There was some blood, but it wasn't aerated and bright like it would be if it had taken a clean shot through the heart and lungs. Luke followed the tracks and drops of blood down the hillside. A quarter mile along the trail, he found where the buck had bedded down. It would have had a direct line of sight to where he had taken his shot. The deer must have gotten up and left when it saw Luke making his way down the mountainside.

About a half hour before dark, he took his headlamp out of his pack and put it in his coat pocket for later. The snow had finally stopped, but he still sank down to just above midcalf with every step. After a mile, the hillside began to level off. A small stream burbled below, flowing gently down towards the flat ground. The amount of the buck's blood never increased or lessened.

The lone beam of his headlamp shone through the trees as he continued to follow the trail. The buck kept bedding down in locations where it could check its back trail, yet if Luke left the deer's trail, he would lose it. His boots were soaked through, and he had long since sweated in his clothes; he chilled down whenever he stopped. He was at least five miles out from his truck, but according to the GPS he had studied before he left, there was a logging road running along the creek that hooked up with the main road.

At eight o'clock, a wall of exhaustion hit him. His shoulders and legs ached from the heavy pack and deep snow, and he felt like he was wading through mud with every step. Luckily, the buck had begun bedding down more frequently and leaving a larger blood trail, a sign that he might be able to catch up to it soon. Luke followed the tracks along a flat area running parallel with the streambed, then decided to see how close the road was to the creek.

He rummaged through his pack and pulled out the GPS. The creek was nowhere on the screen. Weird. Luke pulled out the map, along with the last sandwich. As he ate, he studied the map under the bright circle of light from his headlamp until he found his current location. The blue line of the creek going up the drainage was evident. Looking at the GPS, he saw what should have been the creek outlined in black, indicating a road. A typo. Luke put down the sandwich, his mouth suddenly dry.

Returning what was left of the sandwich to his pack, he considered his options. If he hiked back to the truck now, he would have to walk without resting or risk falling asleep and freezing to death. Then he would have to return to this same spot the next day, and he'd be in almost the same situation as he was now.

The thought of crawling into his warm bed back at the camper was tempting, but the idea of needlessly condemning the buck to a painful and drawn-out death irked him. Not only was it the largest buck he had ever shot, but he couldn't justify giving up the search just when the blood trail had improved. If he went back, it would be at least three or four in the morning before he got there, leaving no time to sleep and recover before he went back out after the buck.

There was another option, yet Luke was reluctant to build the thought into words. He thought of the buck again, slowly dying because his bullet had hit the twig, because of the quick shot, because of him. Dammit! He would have to make a spike camp.

Hastily packing up his gear, he continued down the trail, looking for some sort of start for a shelter or a fire. His feet had lost all feeling while he had been crouched in the snow, and every step landed a second sooner than he expected. Finally, his circulation returned, reclaiming his toes in waves of pain. Luke stomped down the trail through a group of cedars until he came upon a large fallen tree with roots curving out to form a sideways concave bowl. The erosion from previous snowmelts had filled in the space with sand and gravel where the roots had once been, making the ground high enough to prevent being flooded out when the snow melted around his fire.

Luke took a collapsible bow saw from his pack, using the jagged blade rather than the fine-toothed one that was used for cutting bone. He sawed through pine boughs and dragged them back to the uprooted stump, working until he had a pile of wood roughly four feet high. Then noticing a dead ten-foot conifer standing off to the side, its pine needles intact, Luke sawed halfway through, leaned on it until it snapped, and cut the remainder until it was free. He found five more conifers about the same size, cut them, and set them in a pile. He found a flat piece of cedar at the base of where the tree had snapped and fallen, and he broke it from the stump, using it to scrape the snow away from the exposed roots and clearing a seven-by-seven patch of open ground for him and the fire.

Piling the excess snow into a low wall on one side, Luke weaved a few pine boughs through the roots on the other side and above him, then carefully threaded his space blanket through the branches. The rest of the boughs he placed with the branches arching up to form a springy bed away from the frozen ground. The shelter finally ready, he lined up the dead saplings lengthways next to the entrance.

Breaking some of the drier branches apart, Luke organized the twigs into piles of increasing size. He tried lighting the edge of a smaller branch with his cigarette lighter, but the brush was still too wet. He dug around in his pack and found his tinder box. He had stashed it full of dryer lint soaked with petroleum jelly. The lint would serve as a wick, and the Vaseline acted as both wax and fuel. Fluffing the tinder up for more air and surface area, Luke lit the lint.

It flared up, then settled into a low, even flame. Picking up the smallest branches of pine needles, he held them over the tiny flames, close enough to dry and burn but not close enough to smash the tinder and destroy his makings of a fire.

The needles crackled with the heat, and he carefully added twigs, working slowly and giving the fire time to partially dry the twigs before setting them on the fire. The flames eventually gained purchase, and finally, Luke could sit down and dry off. Once he stopped moving, he wanted nothing more than to pass out and sleep like the dead. He didn't really feel hungry, but he finished his sandwich and drank some water anyway. It would be much easier to sleep with food in his stomach.

Luke had always thought it funny when people talked about being too tired to sleep, but he found out it was true. He was sure that he'd fall asleep right away. Instead, he lay half-awake, his eyes closed, gibberish and strange daydreams repeating over and over in his head. It felt like he was walking, yet his feet were completely still, confusing his perception of location and reality. It seemed that every time he dozed off, thinking about his plans for the next day, he got cold and had to stoke up the fire. Eventually, though, he slept.

5

He woke up shivering just before dawn. All that was left of the fire was a pile of hot coals. His hands were dry and stiff from breaking branches in the cold the day before, so he rubbed some snow on them and held them out over the coals to warm while he considered his next steps. He decided to continue tracking the deer until 9:30 and then turn back if he couldn't catch up.

Luke snacked on a Snickers bar and drank the last of his water. He stuffed his canteen full of snow, digging around for the cleaner snow between the surface and the ground. Within minutes, he had packed up his gear, inspected his rifle and scope, and returned to the trail. Although the temperature was probably somewhere in the mid twenties, Luke quickly warmed up, finding his rhythm. Keeping his eyes on the tracks ahead of him, he assessed his situation. He was actually better off than he had first thought. He still had a Snickers bar, a few Cheez-Its, and a sandwich bag filled with dried fruit and nuts. Even if he didn't catch up with his deer by 9:30, he had enough food to trek back to the truck without stopping for too long and freezing, even with one leg of the journey being uphill.

By 8:15, the cedars had given way to twelve-foot willows growing in the midst of snow-covered grass. As he went farther up the side of the creek, he was momentarily blinded by the sunlight reflecting off the snow. Once he adjusted to the brighter light, he noticed that two sets of prints had intercepted his deer's trail from the side of the hill. He thought it was more deer tracks until he saw a large paw print. Wolf. Luke cursed under his breath and quickened his pace. He followed the tracks around a few more turns in the creek, then saw his buck forty yards away, lying in the snow with its antlers sticking out like a patch of heavy brush.

A black wolf with a blaze of white on its chest stood off to the side, its head turned in Luke's direction. Its muzzle was covered with blood. Two more wolves sat on their haunches next to the deer, light gray hides blending in the snow. Luke reached back for his rifle. The wolves, catching his movement, bolted behind the nearest patch of willows and kept going until they were well past the rifle's range.

He pushed forward, keeping an eye on where the wolves had disappeared. As he got close to the buck, he realized his losses were minimal. The wolves had focused on the deer's intestines and a small portion of a hindquarter. They couldn't have been there long. From the tracks, the buck had simply passed away where it had bedded down.

Luke took a moment to marvel at the buck's antlers again. They were six by seven with a tall narrow box and the heavy beams of an older animal. The antlers were almost mahogany, darker than those he was familiar with. Maybe the coloration had to do with the deer population being in the mountains rather than in farmland.

Luke dug his phone out of his pack and took a selfie with the buck, tucking its tongue back into its mouth and angling away from the bloody snow. Then he retrieved his foam pad for a place to sit and ate half of his trail mix and a Snickers bar. Since the snow in his canteen hadn't really melted, he had to eat some clean snow, even though thawing it would use a ton of body heat. Still, he should be plenty warm, now that he was about to begin the real work.

The first step was to finish gutting

the deer. The stomach and intestines were a mess, but the liver was still intact. He would have plenty of weight to haul back already, so he decided to leave it, along with the heart and ribs. Once he rolled the deer on its side, it was ready to move. He would drag the carcass whole to start, then figure out whether to quarter or halve it when he reached the incline to the basin.

Luke shrugged on his backpack and started dragging the deer by the antlers. The snow made the work easier, especially through some of the shorter, denser brush. The buck's carcass left a wide, shallow trail, except wherever a foreleg sank in a softer snow patch. The wolves might be drawn to such an obvious trail, but Luke wasn't too concerned, especially in daylight.

Around noon, after numerous breaks and pauses, the cedars were finally visible. Dragging the buck, combined with not eating much, had slowed Luke down. He realized he wasn't eating enough calories for the cold temperatures and constant exertion. He finished off the trail mix and crumbled Cheez-Its, washing it down with the snow-water from his canteen that had finally melted. He felt like he had just eaten a hearty meal, which wasn't necessarily good because it meant his stomach had shrunk, but he needed to stay positive.

His canteen refilled with snow and

his trash tucked into his backpack, he resumed pulling the buck down the trail. A flash of orange and black caught his eye and he felt lucky to catch a glimpse of a pine marten running through the snow with its weird loping gait before leaping onto some low branches and climbing out of sight. Luke didn't really think of weasels as being a tree climbing animal, yet supposedly squirrels are their prey of choice. Dang squirrels. He wished it luck.

By two o'clock, Luke had just about reached the spike camp. He paused to consider. He still had a long way to go. The hillside going back up to the basin was too steep to drag the deer up whole, so he would need to quarter the buck and carry out half at a time. No way would he be able to get one of the halves back to his camper today, so he decided to use the remaining daylight to butcher the carcass and improve his shelter. The temperature had risen to somewhere in the low thirties, so Luke would probably be able to get some sleep, especially if he added more pine boughs to his shelter.

He took out his bow saw and cut down ten of the small trees that had died last winter but remained standing and dry. He had to go farther from the camp, since he had cut the closest ones the day before. Collecting pine boughs was easier, and by dusk he had a four-foot pile next to his shelter. He built a platform over the dead coals of his fire using three of the trees he had just cut. Then he piled some branches on top and ignited a clump of nearby lichen to get the fire going.

With the blaze throwing light in all corners of the camp, Luke went to work on the deer. He started by skinning out the front right quarter, then followed the seams of connective tissue between the shoulder and torso until it was cut free. He stowed the freshly cut meat in a game bag. He did the same with the left foreleg, then carved out the tenderloins or *filet mignon*, as some people called them, from along the spine opposite the backstrap. He set the tenderloin pieces on makeshift skewers over the fire. Then he stepped out of the camp area to stretch his back and look at the sky.

The cloud cover kept any light from the night sky hidden. That was a blessing in a way because the overcast sky would hold in the heat. The woods around his island of light were pitch black and silent. No doubt animals weren't active now because they couldn't see very much either. When the fire snapped, he returned to the camp and rotated his steaks.

He went back to work on the buck, skinning out the back and hindquarters. He cut out the backstraps, tucking the hide underneath the deer to keep the meat out of the snow. He put the steaks in the same game bag as the front quarters, leaving the hindquarters in a separate game bag. Then he sawed off the part of the legs between the hoof and second joint. Since that part of the animal was only bone, hair, and tendon, there was no reason to carry the extra weight.

Since he planned to do a European mount, he cut the vertebrae closest to the skull to keep the weight down. He carved out the larger pieces of neck meat for stew and hamburger. Luke added these cuts to the bag with the front quarters, then hauled it to a tree at the edge of the camp. He'd need to hang the bags in the trees to keep animals away from his deer overnight while he slept and tomorrow while he was gone. Using twenty feet of parachute cord and tying a slipknot over the opening, Luke tossed the bag over the highest branch possible, pulled it up, and tied the line off. The hindquarters were heavier, but they went up the same way. Finally, he was ready to check on his fire and shelter.

The steaks were sizzling and ready. He picked up one skewer and set the other on the far edge of the coals to stay warm, then flopped down onto the pile of pine boughs he had created. The branches were flexible enough that they formed a crude Adirondack armchair. Luke broke off one end of the skewer and began eating the steak as if it were corn on the cob. Afterwards, he sat for a time, soaking in the novelty of the moment.

But as with all things, the moment couldn't last. The steak made him thirsty, so he brought his pack to his branch chair and rummaged through it until he found his canteen. The melted snow in the flask only gave up about a cup and a half of water. He found his empty soda can, cut off the top few centimeters with his least favorite knife blade, filled it snow, and set it on the edge of the fire, adding more snow as the water warmed. Within a few minutes, he had water to go with his steaks and enough to refill his canteen as long as he was quick enough to prevent the heat going through his insulated gloves and burning him.

Luke stoked up the fire and sat staring into the flames. His belly was full of steak, and all he wanted to do now was to fall asleep on his warm chair of pine boughs by the fire. But the fire would die down and he'd wake up again in an hour, so he added more branches to his shelter, using the driest ones for his bed and the wetter ones to better seal up the walls. The snow wall that he had built was beginning to melt, so he scraped it smooth with the back of his hand to reduce the surface area exposed to air. He banked the fire, crawled into his shelter, unfolded his space blanket, and fell fast sleep.

6

Luke woke up at first light and brought the fire up to a steady blaze. He had only stoked the fire once during the night, so there was plenty of firewood left. Once he had warmed up again, he stood studying the game bags, contemplating his next move. He had to decide which bag to carry with him on the first trip to the truck. The larger bag with the two hindquarters weighed roughly the same as the bag with the rest of the deer, including the antlers—which were surprisingly heavy and unwieldy with the skull and part of the hide still attached.

In the end, Luke decided to play a game with himself: he would leave the antlers hanging with the remainder of the buck at the spike camp. He had never planned on making only one trip and leaving the rest of the deer behind, yet he decided to do things this way as a sort of self-motivation failsafe. He shrugged his shoulders as if to defend his decision, then untied the larger game bag from the tree. Taking some of the pine boughs from his shelter, he reached up and set them over the second game bag to keep the birds off.

The hindquarters weren't fully frozen yet, so Luke cut a dozen thin slices from the area he had cut earlier because of the wolves. He skewered the slices and set them as close to the fire as he could without burning the thin stakes of wood. The slices began sizzling within minutes. Meanwhile, he packed up camp and, using parachute cord, created double loops around the large game bag, wrapping green twigs around them to cushion his hands and shoulders. Finally ready to roll, he took the four least-cooked slices of meat off the fire to eat right away and set the other eight aside to cool. Luke ate as quickly as he could without burning himself then stuffed the remainder in his old sandwich bag. He kicked the burning firewood off to the edges of the fire so he could use them later if he needed to.

Luke shouldered his pack, checked his rifle, and hefted the game bag by its loops. It would have been easier to carry the quarters using his metal pack frame, but it was back at the truck, and carrying the bag without one would be better than making an extra trip. The first hundred feet were the most difficult as he warmed up and figured out the best way to carry the bag. While stopping to catch his breath, he lengthened the loops around the quarters, which made it possible to carry it on top of his pack against the back of his neck, as long as he kept tension on the loops with his arms. Carrying the game bag was much easier like this, but he doubted that he would be able to get away with climbing the steeper mountainside on the way to the basin without at least one hand free.

Now that he had a system and had caught his second wind, he made good time through the cedars along the creek. Around 8:30, he stopped at the base of the hillside. The sky was clear and cloudless with an almost metallic blue tint. Without the cloud cover from the night before, the temperature had dropped.

Luke shifted the weight of the bag to his left shoulder and slowly made his way up the hillside, using his free arm to grab brush and pull himself up. Rocks and slippery brush were hidden beneath the snow, and he picked his way carefully to keep his footing. The quarters kept him off-balance, and he hitched up his right shoulder to keep his gun sling from falling off.

The effort of climbing the hill with the heavy game bag forced Luke to stop and catch his breath every twenty yards. When he had climbed roughly two-thirds of the way up, he looked back. The darker green of the cedars along the creek gradually gave way to the lighter brown and white of the willows in the distant snowfield. It had been a good morning's work.

7

Luke reached the edge of the bowl at

noon. After snacking on some venison and water, he rewrapped his parachute cord back into makeshift straps and continued along the edge of the basin. It had taken him longer than expected to reach this point, but he was optimistic that he would make better time, now that he was on level ground. He knew where he was going so he trudged along with his head down, glancing up occasionally to get his bearings or glare at a chattering squirrel.

Every time he stopped to rest, he chilled down, so mostly he stopped only to eat or drink, and only when he had to. He had gone through all of the water that he had melted at the spike camp, and thawing new snow in his canteen yielded mostly slush. His gums were painful and bleeding from chewing the tough venison strips.

CRACK. THUD. Luke spun around with his rifle in ready position, just in time to see a tree crash twenty yards behind him. Some of the dense standing timber was dead so falling trees were a surprisingly fairly common occurrence, yet they still scared the crap out of him every time. Grinning to himself at his exhibition of nerves, he kept pushing forward until he made it to the beginning of the ridgeline.

When he reached the ridgeline, he shifted to walking downhill. It was faster, even with the extra weight of the game bag, but it required more effort than flatter terrain. Luke had to fight gravity with each step to keep from slipping downhill at a stumbling run.

He stopped to rest his burning leg muscles. A clearing was visible through gaps between trees. It had to be the right clearing, even though it seemed smaller than he remembered, because after a few more minutes of walking, he was standing in front of his truck and camper.

A wave of relief washed over him. He swiped the snow off a nearby log with his free arm and set down the game bag. He unlocked the camper and stowed his gun and backpack inside. Then he climbed in, lit all three propane burners for warmth, and sat down to snack on chips and salsa. Reaching for the radio, he searched for a station, stopping when he found a station playing Credence Clearwater Revival. With music playing, the camper suddenly felt warmer and more homelike—the feeling from sitting next to a campfire, but different.

With the salsa nearly finished and the camper warmed up, Luke kept on falling asleep and waking up the second his head would hit his shoulder. Before he went to sleep for the night, he needed to replace the calories he had burned. He put a can of soup into a pot with the burner on low and set his watch alarm for 10 minutes. The beeping of the alarm jarred him awake. He sidled along the cramped booth of the camper and took the boiling soup off the burner. While it cooled, he grabbed his headlamp and stepped outside to hang up the deer quarters for the night.

Choosing a secure branch, Luke hoisted up the game bag and looped some rope around the trunk. When a chill ran between his shoulders, he realized he was standing outside wearing only his flannel instead of a jacket. Before he climbed back into the camper, he turned his headlamp off and looked up. Stars gleamed in the gaps between the trees, promising another cold night. A quick step onto a five-gallon bucket, and Luke was back to the warmth of the camper.

He reheated the cooled-down soup while he changed into his lounging clothes. There was no getting used to warming up blankets and sleeping bags when cold, so he fluffed them up a bit in hopes that the warm air from the burners would transfer some of their heat. He scarfed down the soup while studying the map and tracing his route from over the past few days. He grabbed his GPS and vehemently tossed it in the corner. The soup gone, he checked his watch: eight o'clock. He set his alarm for five o'clock and hoped nine hours would be enough sleep.

At five, the alarm beeped, snapping the new day sharply in focus. He dragged himself out of his sleeping bag only after he thought about his deer being picked at by birds and other animals. Once he was up, he struggled to move against the aches and pains that had accumulated over the past few days.

He heated up some hash browns for breakfast. He made four sandwiches for the hike, packed extra Gatorade, and filled his canteen. As he hefted up his backpack, he chipmunked as much of the hash browns into his cheeks as he could, then folded the rest into a slice of bread to eat as he walked.

Luke stepped out of the camper and

checked his gear, then his watch: 5:32 a.m. Since he'd already shot his buck, he would bring his .44 revolver instead of the heavier rifle. A glow from the east gave him just enough light to discern the clear-cut from the rest of the ridge. He glanced quickly at the mountain before making his way back up the trail.

The temperature was in the low twenties, cooling him enough to minimize his breaks. It felt strange tying his backpack to the top of the pack frame, but it was much lighter without the saw and his other gear. When he arrived back at the spike camp, Luke was relieved to see that the remaining game bag was undisturbed.

8

By two o'clock, the sun had moved halfway across the sky. He didn't have much daylight left. Working the first quarter's knot loose, he swiftly lowered the game bag and laid it down on top of his pack frame. The next quarter's knot was too tight, so still holding the rope with his right hand, he deftly opened his pocketknife with the other and hopped on a log with one foot to cut the cord higher and save rope. As he reached to make the cut, his footing gave way and he fell forward. The blade of his knife sliced the palm of his left hand, ripping skin from muscle.

Luckily, the blood oozed at a heavy, steady pace. If a vein had been cut, the blood would be gushing. Luke sank to his knees in the snow, immediately applying pressure with his other hand to stop the bleeding. When that didn't work, he pressed his injured hand against his leg while he cautiously poked around underneath his coat with his knife to cut his T-shirt off. Working slowly and awkwardly with his one good hand, he tore the cloth into strips for bandages. Then he wrapped the makeshift bandage around his injured hand, tying it off with parachute cord. Finally, the flow of blood ebbed.

Now that the immediate danger had passed, his brain was free enough for thoughts to creep in. "What did I do? WHAT DID I DO?" The words pounded through his head like a runaway train. As he regained control of his emotions, he realized it could have been much worse.

Blood splatter stained the snow around him. Getting back to the truck was now his highest priority. But first he had to get the game bag back up in the air to keep the meat out of reach of other animals. The rope was still tied to the bag, so Luke tossed the rope over the branch and hoisted it up as far as he could by setting his weight against it. He was unable to tie a knot, but the bag held after several wraps around a broken lower branch.

Luke shouldered his pack frame on, wincing as the wound in his hand reopened and then resealed itself. He struggled climbing up to the basin. With only one hand for balance and his legs jittery, he fell twice, causing his wound to start bleeding again, seeping through the wrapping. Reluctantly, Luke cut off a few strips of his flannel shirt and wrapped the cloth around the bloody bandage. As much as he wanted to remove the soiled bandages, he had heard somewhere that it was better to leave them on and just add new ones.

Once again on level ground, Luke moved quickly through the groves of trees along the basin, stopping occasionally to pack snow around his bandage until he realized that it was only soaking up blood and falling off, as well as making his fingers numb. Hunger forced him to stop and eat. He shrugged off his frame crouched down and dug through his pack until he found a ham sandwich. The bread was thoroughly squashed yet surprisingly delicious as he fumbled with the sandwich bag. Kneeling over his pack instantly eased the pain in his back. He didn't recall when it had started hurting.

The dwindling light pushed him back to his feet. He needed to get back to his truck and find someone to stitch up his hand. He stepped to the other side of his pack, away from the bloody snow that had accumulated while he rested. Glancing up, he locked eyes with a mountain lion only twenty steps away.

The lion, realizing it had been spotted, froze in midstep, shoulders low and primed for movement. Its pupils were dilated and seemed to see everything around with an impartial intensity, all while locking eyes with Luke's in an unwavering glare. Was it going to pounce? Run away? Was it going to sneak up on him again if he let it leave? The cougar sat on its haunches and continued to stare, its tail twitching almost imperceptibly.

Luke's revolver was tucked securely in the holster underneath his coat. Any quick-draw tricks were going to be slow with cold and bandaged hands. He squared up his center of gravity to resist a spring from the lion. His good hand slowly reached for the gun. The lion tenuously backed up, then turned and slinked away through the trees. Luke drew his revolver and fired at the cougar's outline as it flitted through the trees. The gun's concussion echoed and then faded, leaving the forest quieter than before.

9

Darkness fell as he made his way down the ridgeline. Luke glanced behind him periodically to make sure the mountain lion hadn't followed him. The trail was clear, and soon his truck lit up in the glow of his headlamp.

Setting his gear down and climbing into the camper, he worked on his bandages. The wound was still seeping, so he replaced all but the first layer of wraps with a towel and then tied everything off with a piece of truck strap. He must have lost more blood than he thought because the camper was spinning and he felt sick. Or maybe it was just the shock of recent events rather than actual blood loss.

Around nine o'clock, Luke fired up the truck. The frozen camper jacks had to be persuaded with a hammer, then with the valves shut and tied off he was finally ready to go, keeping his injured hand tucked against his chest. He rolled out onto the road and made his way down the mountain, the windows rolled down and the radio blasting to keep himself awake.

By the time he got into town and found the urgent care center, little more than an hour had passed. He parked and climbed into the camper to sleep until the facility opened at five. He set the alarm for 4:30, but before it woke him, he was startled by a sharp rap on the camper door. Luke snapped awake, kicked on a pair of sweatpants, and swung the door open. A heavyset man with white curly hair and glasses stood outside, his hands in the pockets of his ski jacket.

"I'm Dr. Reynolds. You seem like you might be impatiently waiting for us to open," he said with a laugh. "How can we help you?"

Luke held up his injured hand sheepishly.

"Yeowch. Come inside when you're ready, and we'll get you patched up. When Olivia gets here, she'll give you some forms to fill out."

"Sweet. I'm Luke. Thanks for letting me in early," he replied.

Olivia's description could only be summed up in a single word. Sassy. When she arrived, she sauntered past him in the waiting room and dug around behind the counter. Her electric blue highlights were just visible through strands of brown hair. "What did you do?" she asked in a mock accusing tone as she slid the paperwork across the counter.

Luke told his story from the beginning while he filled out the paperwork, even the parts that sounded made up or stupid. When Dr. Reynolds called him back, Olivia went, too. By the time Luke finished his story, his hand had been sewn up. Both Olivia and Dr. Reynolds looked at him with blank expressions, and Luke couldn't tell if they thought he was lying or crazy. Dr. Reynolds spoke first: "Glad you're back in one piece, young man," Dr. Reynolds said then left to see to his next patient.

Olivia walked back with him to the front. "I liked your story," she said."I'd like to hear it again. Let me know if you need anything else." She gave him a card, and then turned to help the next patient. Luke tucked the card in his pocket. Maybe he would give her a call.

It was Friday, so Luke called Sean while he had reception but got no answer.

"He must've lost his Bluetooth." Luke figured as he headed back up the road towards camp. He parked, lowered the camper jacks, and made sandwiches for the next day. The venison quarters were still undisturbed, so Luke curled up in the camper to sleep.

He woke to headlights shining in his camper around seven and recognized the sound of Sean's truck. After throwing some clothes on and lighting the lantern, Luke started digging through his gear until he found his cards and cribbage board. He could hear the crunching of approaching footsteps and then the door swung open.

Moments later, Sean leaned his lanky

form into the camper. "You're still here?" he asked, handing Luke a bottle of whiskey.

Luke laughed. "There were a few delays." Over the next few hours, Luke told him the whole story while they played cribbage and listened to the radio.

"You should have tried to fight the cougar, Luke. That would have been badass."

"I thought about it," Luke replied. "It was probably only about 120 pounds, but it also had claws. So the way I see it, it would be like fighting some small guy that runs around killing deer with knives all the time. No thank you."

Sean choked on the barbecue chips

he was eating.

They made their way up the ridge just after dawn. Luke carried his revolver while Sean had his rifle in case he saw any deer. When they passed where Luke had seen the cougar, Sean paced out the distances and took pictures of the prints. When they reached the spike camp, he looked over the shelter Luke had put together. Then he pulled down the game bag that contained the other half of the buck and measured the deer's antlers with his hands. "Dang! This almost seems worth it," he said, his eyes widening

They split up the weight between them for the return trip. By seven o'clock, the entire buck had been loaded into Luke's camper. They stood in front of the trucks looking at the forest around them for a minute. Then Luke shook Sean's hand and said with a grin, "Good luck, man. Don't steal my spot," he said with a grin.

Luke's truck clawed its way through the snow until he made it to blacktop. Any more snow and it would have been rough driving out. It looked like the roads would be clear for Sean, though; the weather forecast was for clear skies the rest of the week. Luke pushed down on the gas pedal. He had a lot of work to do when he got home. His buck wasn't going to climb into the freezer on its own.